About *Benji's Christmas Letter*

This story is so touching and so full of love from every angle. *Benji's Christmas Letter* is the kind of story anyone can relate to who knows how it is to miss someone. Every line is a little more compelling and builds suspense to such a sweet ending. I can see how this one could be read every Christmas as a family tradition, renewing the spirit of hope, wishes, giving, and small miracles that mean so much!

—Catherine Bosley, News anchor, WOIO Channel 19, Cleveland, OH

Benji's Christmas Letter

Andrea Baker

tate publishing
CHILDREN'S DIVISION

Published by Tate Publishing & Enterprises, LLC
127 E. Trade Center Terrace | Mustang, Oklahoma 73064 USA
1.888.361.9473 | www.tatepublishing.com

Tate Publishing is committed to excellence in the publishing industry. The company reflects the philosophy established by the founders, based on Psalm 68:11,
"The Lord gave the word and great was the company of those who published it."

Book design copyright © 2012 by Tate Publishing, LLC. All rights reserved.
Cover and interior design by Errol Villamante
Illustrations by Jason Hutton

Published in the United States of America

ISBN: 978-1-62295-005-8
1. Juvenile Fiction / Family / Parents
2. Juvenile Fiction / Fairy Tales & Folklore / General
12.10.05

Benji's
Christmas Letter

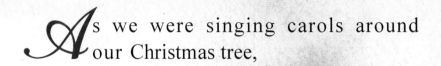

As we were singing carols around our Christmas tree,

Benji stopped his singing and slowly turned to me.

"Mommy," he said, in a voice soft and sweet.

What would he ask? My heart skipped a beat.

"I want to write a letter." Then he gave me a smile.

"I will need you to help me, and it might take us a while."

"Of course," I said. "But who is it for?"

I was sure it was for his dad, who was off in the war.

"Mommy," he said, "it's to Santa, you see.

I want a special gift, but not just for me."

So, we stopped what we were doing and grabbed the paper and pen.

We started the Christmas letter for little Benji to send.

DEAR SAN

"Oh, my dearest Santa Claus, do you remember me?

It was about a year ago when I sat upon your knee.

I asked you for a Christmas gift, and it brought me a lot
of joy.

I asked for the meaning of Christmas, and you told me
of a boy.

I know that he is special, and I keep him in my heart.

But maybe you can tell him there are families torn apart.

There are a lot of moms and dads that have been sent off to war.

I know that it's important, but I can't take it anymore.

You see, my daddy is a soldier, and he's been gone for quite a while.

I wish that he could be here so I could see my mommy smile.

She tries to hide her tears from me, and she is my saving grace.

I know her heart is breaking although she wears her bravest face.

If I could ask for one more gift, I would ask
you to end this fight.

So our soldiers and their families could be
together every night.

It hurts to know he's far from home and the
pain is oh so deep.

I lie awake in bed at night and wonder where
he sleeps.

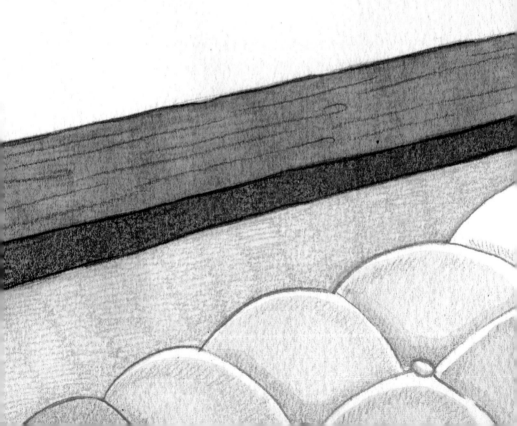

You see, my daddy is my hero, and to me, he is the best.

Because of soldiers like my daddy, the world is truly blessed.

I know that there are a lot of kids who feel the same as me.

We know our parents fight the fight to keep us safe and free.

I know you will do your best to bring this
  gift to me

because Christmas is a special time, and in
  my heart, I do believe.

But if you cannot bring my daddy home,
  please keep him safe from harm.

And I will pray every night 'til he can hold
  me in his arms.

So, my dearest Santa Claus, my Christmas wish
is this.

Please bring our soldiers back home to us, for
they are deeply missed."

When I woke up Christmas morning, I ran
down to the tree,

There stood the greatest gift, waiting just
for me!

My daddy came home! Even if only for
a while,

Santa fulfilled my Christmas wish, and I saw
my mommy smile.

Christmas is a magical time when miracles
do come true,

Thank you, dear Santa Claus, for everything
you do!

e|LIVE

---

listen|imagine|view|experience

AUDIO BOOK DOWNLOAD INCLUDED WITH THIS BOOK!

In your hands you hold a complete digital entertainment package. In addition to the paper version, you receive a free download of the audio version of this book. Simply use the code listed below when visiting our website. Once downloaded to your computer, you can listen to the book through your computer's speakers, burn it to an audio CD or save the file to your portable music device (such as Apple's popular iPod) and listen on the go!

How to get your free audio book digital download:

1. Visit www.tatepublishing.com and click on the e|LIVE logo on the home page.
2. Enter the following coupon code:
   8071-57e3-4f4a-dd1e-47d1-d3c4-fdab-145c
3. Download the audio book from your e|LIVE digital locker and begin enjoying your new digital entertainment package today!